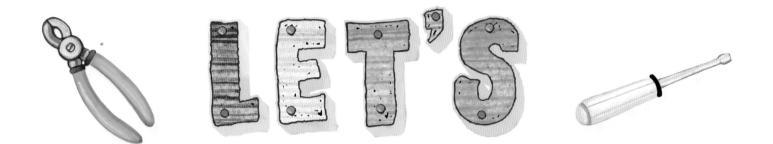

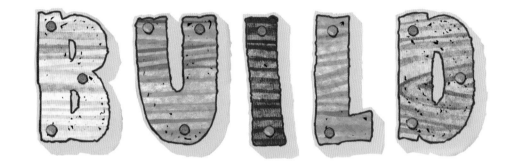

LET'S BUILD

by

Sue Fliess

illustrated by

Miki Sakamoto

two lions

To Mom and Dad, for helping me build my dreams
—S.F.

Was thinking of you, Dad, while I created the images for this book.
I love you always!!
—M.S.

two lions

Text copyright © 2014 Sue Fliess
Illustrations copyright © 2014 Miki Sakamoto
All rights reserved.

ISBN-13: 9781477847244
ISBN-10: 1477847243

Published by Two Lions, New York
www.apub.com

Amazon, the Amazon logo, and Two Lions are trademarks of Amazon.com, Inc., or its affiliates.

The illustrations were rendered in gouache and acrylics and then altered in Photoshop.
Book design by Vera Soki

Printed in China
First edition

It's the weekend.

Time to play?

Yes, let's build
a fort today!

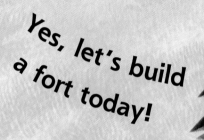

Choose the best spot
in our yard.
Gus will be our trusty guard.

Grab a pencil,
draw the plans.
We'll construct it with our hands.

Make a checklist.
Search the aisles.
Hardware stores
go on for miles!

Here's a handsaw,
bolts and screws.
Look! Some plywood
we can use.

Paints and brushes,
drill bits, wires,
hammer, nails,
a pair of pliers.

Mark and measure,

cut and sand.

Lay the floor—now we can stand.

"Time to hammer."
"Swing it now?"
"Wait! Here, let me
show you how."

Raise the walls up.
Hoist that beam.
Real construction takes a team!

Mac and cheese and cake to share.

Back to business,
tummies full.
Energy to lift and pull.

Set the roof on.
Almost done . . .
Two big windows let in sun.

There's a hole.
What's it for?
"Look, Gus, it's
your special door!"

Paint the outside
blue and red.
Oops! I dripped some on Dad's head!

Secret password,
handshake, too—
learn them and
I'll let you through.

We'll play board games,
draw and write . . .

Can we sleep in here tonight?

MEMBERS ONLY!

"Here's your
clubhouse."
What a crew!
"It's for us, Dad—me and you."